Bears in a Band

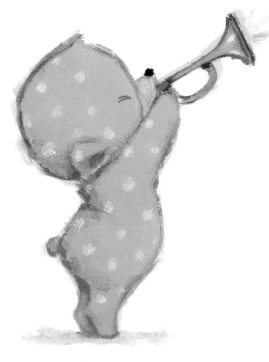

Shirley Parenteau
illustrated by David Walker

WALKER BOOKS
AND SUBSIDIARIES

LONDON · BOSTON · SYDNEY · AUCKLAND

Music makers
are on the chairs.
Is there a band?
Where are the bears?

Here they come.
"Music! Hooray!"
Each bear chooses
something to play.

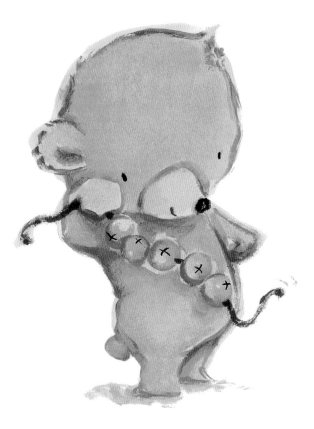

Yellow Bear likes
bells on a string.
He makes them dance.
Ding-a-ding-ding!

WOW!

Floppy Bear pounds
a shiny red drum.

Boompity boomp!

Pah-rum, pum, pum!

A golden horn
for Calico.
Tootley-tooo!
Fast, then slow!

Fuzzy likes to
crash and bang.
She picks up cymbals.
Clang! Clang! Clang!

The bears all play
a noisy song.

They don't care
if the notes are wrong.

SNORE!
Is someone sleeping?
Big Brown Bear!
Will he hear
the band prepare?

The drumbeat BANGS!
The music LEAPS.
The noise rolls in
where Big Bear sleeps.

Uh-oh!
Big Bear sits up.
His blanket falls.
"What's going on?"
the big bear calls.

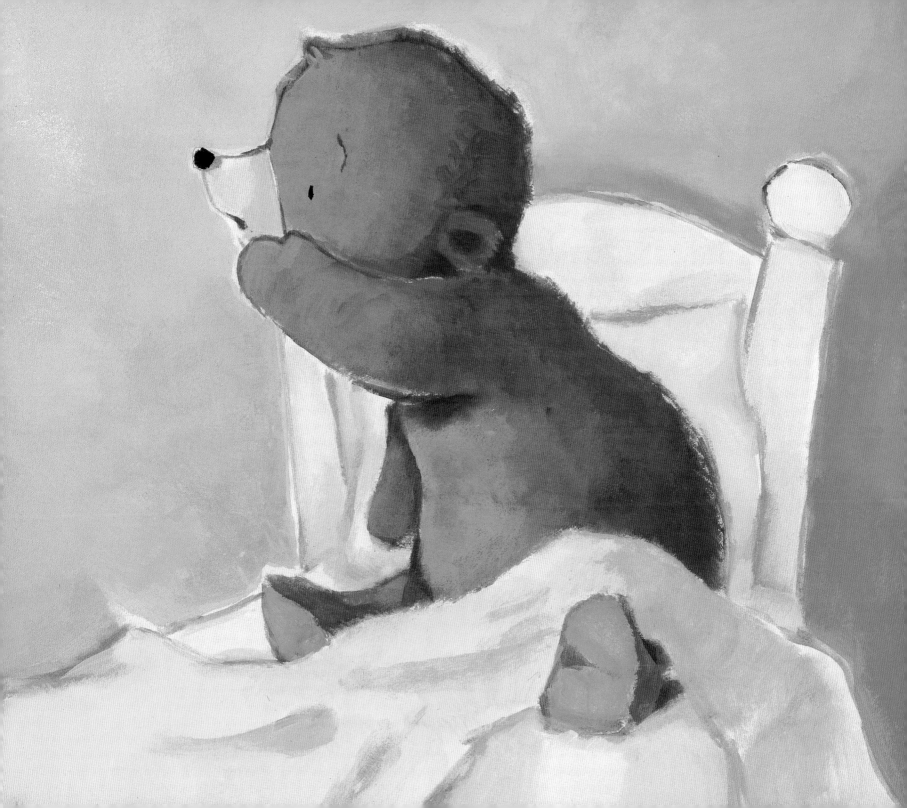

PUM-PAH-RUM!

RING-a-ding-DONG!

That's not music.

Something is wrong!

The big bear rushes
into the room.
The racket stops
with a small *ka-boom*.

Look!

He picks up a ladle.

Is the big bear mad?

No, he's grinning.

The big bear's glad.

He joins the others
on dancing feet
with his ladle baton
setting the beat.

"Softer on the drum."
The ladle moves slow.

"Louder on the bells."
See the ladle go!

When Big Brown Bear
leads the little bear band,
they all play together
and the harmony is grand!

A ripple of bells,
a drum roll and now
the musical bears
share an elegant bow.

For my musical granddaughters: Michelle, Nicole and
Elizabeth on piano and Carole, who chose the harp
S. P.

Especially for Lori and the guitar she's determined to master!
D. W.

First published 2016 by Walker Books Ltd
87 Vauxhall Walk, London SE11 5HJ

2 4 6 8 10 9 7 5 3 1

Text © 2016 Shirley Parenteau
Illustrations © 2016 David Walker

This book was typeset in Journal

Printed in China

British Library Cataloguing in Publication Data:
A catalogue record for this book is available from the British Library

ISBN 978-1-4063-7268-7

www.walker.co.uk